PIRATE TREASURE

Published in 2009 by Windmill Books, LLC
303 Park Avenue South, Suite # 1280, New York, NY 10010-3657

Series Editor: Nick Turpin
Design: Robert Walster
Production: Jenny Mulvanny

Publisher Cataloging Data

Anderson, Scoular
     Pirate treasure / by Scoular Anderson.
          p. cm. – (Get set readers)
     Summary: A pirate captain finds a treasure map but has problems finding the treasure.
     ISBN 978-1-60754-266-7
     1. Pirates—Juvenile fiction   2. Treasure troves—Juvenile fiction
[1. Pirates—Fiction   2. Buried treasure—Fiction   3. Maps—Fiction]   I. Title
II. Series
     [E]—dc22

Manufactured in the United States of America

PIRATE TREASURE

by Scoular Anderson

alphabet
s o u p
an imprint of

WINDMILL
BOOKS
New York

When the pirate captain
opened his chest...

...looking for socks and
an itchy vest...

...he found – a map!

He ran to his crew...

9

"You know what to do
with this wonderful clue –
it's time to hunt for treasure."

11

So they sailed away...

12

...to a wide, sandy bay...

13

...to dig in the sand.

The sand piled up as they dug for loot...

16

17

...but they found no treasure,
just a smelly old boot!

The captain cried, "It's just not fair!"
Then stamped his foot and pulled his hair.

21

The cabin boy looked at the map…

...first like
this, then
like that.

23

At last he told them with
a frown,
"The treasure map was
upside down!"

They raced away to
dig again.

This time the captain did not complain!

29

Then each pirate wore a smile,
when each pirate had a pile
of bright and shiny pirate gold.

For more great fiction and nonfiction, go to www.windmillbks.com.